Chapter 1

"The unidentified man was found by a member of the public, who had been out walking his dog along by the duck pond in Newtownards…"

I paused and looked up from the newspaper,

"Fuckin' hell love, they've found another one," I shouted across the kitchen to Pavla.

"Shhhhhh," she scolded, plucking Skye up from her high chair and covering her ears,

"She will repeat it Jim."

"Jeez", I said, rolling my eyes, "here, listen to this," I added, searching for the spot,

"The unnamed man's head was almost severed from his body and a large portion of skin had been removed from one of his fingers."

I looked up, shaking my head,

"Bloody hell, that's the third one."

"Ah-ah!" Pavla rasped sharply, then breezed out with Skye on her shoulder.

"I didn't say fuck," I called after her.

Chapter 2

I was gulping down my second coffee of the day when my first customer rolled in. It was near eleven. My mind had been drifting back to the morning paper, and I was thinking how there were some sick puppies about in this old world. Pav had put Skye down for a nap and we had breakfast together; she hadn't been really that pissed off with me. I made us my speciality scrambled eggs, with extra buttery toast, so she had to at least be civil. Anyways, I suppose I should introduce myself a little. No actually I won't; if you don't know who I am, you should have bought my first fucking book.

"Brian, how are you mate?"

"Not bad Jim, Baltic out there today buddy."

He wasn't actually a customer, so much as a salesperson, or even a stakeholder if you will. Brian helped me out with shifting some of my gear. Gear of the green variety. He pulled his tattered old 'Norn Iron' cap off and revealed his greying and receding locks.

"Cuppa mate?" I asked.

"Always," he said, rubbing his hands.

After I had a brew with Brian, he took a few baggies to sell and headed on. I did a wee tidy up round the store, had a wipe round and that, which resulted in me mostly just strumming a couple of my best guitars. I tuned the sunburst Les Paul to *DADGAD* and tried a bit of 'Stairway to Heaven.' I fiddled about for a few minutes. It's a fucking embarrassment that I still can't nail the intro. Maybe it'd be easier in *Open G*. Fuck it. I set it down and decided to try and find the vacuum. The summer holidays were coming and I thought there'd hopefully be an increase in school kids coming in for strings and even a few records. Well, I was an optimist at least. It was also about a year after the whole thing with Davy Dick. God rest him- I suppose. A few more customers trickled in and out again. Most of them didn't buy anything- it fucking cracks me up. I thought about getting some tablature books in- just so I could say, 'This is not a library.' Anyway, all in all things were pretty sweet with my little life. The shop was surviving, people still needed me to sell them some grass, Skye had started playgroup, and Pav was nearly done with her NVQ or QCF thing. I still got to keep 'Bongo Fury'; my sanctum, my piece of- and peace *from* the world.

After dinner that night, I left my girls watching C-Beebies and scooted out to see my brother Leo. Me and him had been meeting up more regularly again, having a few drinks like brothers are meant to.

"Pint?" I asked unnecessarily.

"Cheers Jim, I'll get us a wee short to go with it."

"Okay, I better leave my fucking car then," I said and turned to the waitress, "Two Harps please love."

We decided to hook up in *Wolseys*- neither of us had gone there in years, taking our drinks to a corner snug. We had found ourselves in the habit of going to places where Leo shouldn't be too likely to bump into 'work colleagues.' He had risen up the ranks a brave bit recently and from what I gathered, he had quite a bit of responsibility. I tried not to ask too many questions- I didn't much want to know. We got comfy and I threw my coat over the back of the booth. My ears pricked up to the sounds of some early Prince coming over the bar speakers. Involuntarily, my head started to bob.

"Bloody new suit again brother," I said, taking my first cool and satisfyingly bubbly sip.

"Surprised you'd notice, you scruffy bastard," he said, smirking.

I looked down at my Led Zep T-shirt and 'go-to' blue jeans. I shrugged. He was in a full blue suit, striped, with a tie and everything. Until recently I had only caught him in a full tie and suit at funerals- or in court. On reflection, both had been reasonably regular occurrences.

"How's your clan?" I asked.

"Jesus," he said with a shake, "bloody kids, if I have to go to one more teacher meeting about Blake's behaviour." He pulled at his tie and took a long slug.

We talked for a bit about the kids, Bongo Fury; the usual shit. He seemed in good form, calm, not too sarky. The moody bastard was in good form. That restless spirit of his seemed to be finally settling down a bit too. Fair play to him I reckoned.

"We'll have to get a wee night out with the wives- get babysitters- no kids," he added, starting on his short. He had bought us both a Black Bush.

"Absolutely- just say when, things are pretty quiet our end."

"Yeah actually," he said, pulling at his tie again, with his forehead creasing, "Things are a wee touch mad at the minute- I've some business shit to get sorted out- it'll be better in a wee bit. Might need to leave it a week or two."

"Dead on- just when suits," I said.

“Fuck, this place sure has changed, hasn’t it?” said Leo, looking round, “They’ve done it up- must have cost some.”
“Yeah,” I said, following where his gaze had rested, “It used to be dark and a bit friggen dingy,” I added, then emptying my glass, “It was better like that.”
He tutted
“Well- ‘nother round?” I enquired.
“Go on- a short for me. Just going for a smoke,” he said rising, slipping out of the booth and then checking his phone. He made a face, then shuffled on outside.

Chapter 3

I was greeted by newly hung bunting on my way into work the next day. Union flags and UVF banners had sprung up- engulfing the estates and everywhere in between. It was if I was Union Jack himself and they had been put out for my birthday. Maybe it was a present from my brother. The thought made me smile. We were approaching July and the period where hard core Prods felt the need to piss all over their territory. I'm a Unionist, many in my family have fucking died for being Unionists; I'm more connected that a fucking Connect-4. But, to me, I think 'fucking easy on boyos.' I like The Union, but I like The Beatles too. I just don't feel the need to drape Beatles flags outside my house, and my neighbours' house, and to set fire to flags of The Rolling Stones.

It was already nine when I got to my shop, take-out coffee in hand. Two men in grey suits were standing outside my shutter. I had been late before, but had never found customers waiting on me. I slowed my steps and eyed them as I rustled in my pockets for my keys. The first man was stocky, chewing hard on some gum, making a face like the gum tasted of aniseed. I bloody hate aniseed. The second was a touch older, taller and leaner. He nodded and gave me a sideways smile.

"Ahh," I said dramatically, "You two must be queuing for the 'One Direction' tickets, isn't it great that the lads are back together?"

I started to pull up the shutter, almost shoving 'Sour Face' out the way. The second man kept smiling,

"Hello Jimmy, very droll, we'd like a word in your ear."

"Certainly," I said, opening the inside door, "Come through, I am here for all your vinyl and musical instrument queries."

I switched on the lights and walked through, then positioned myself behind the counter. It felt better there, I was in charge whatever this was, it was my shop after all. The last time two fellas came in like this, I smashed a pink ukulele over one of their thick heads. I let these two amble in behind me.

"We're police, this…"

"No shit," I interrupted, offering up my finest unimpressed face.

"I am D.I Merritt, this is D.S Timmons," he continued passively.

I shrugged and let out a yawn.

"Look, is there somewhere quiet we can go?" broke in Timmons.

"Is it not quiet enough here? It's not my busy time," I added and shot him a sarcastic smile.

"Fine," said Merritt, his patience dwindling a touch, "It's up to you. It's also up to you if we arrest you for possession and sale of a Class B drug.

"I don't know what you're talking about," I answered, far too quickly.

"C'man Jimmy, don't fuck around," began Timmons aggressively, "We haven't the time for it."

Timmons' face had started to purple. Merritt creased his forehead at his colleague, then returned his gaze to me,

"We know all about your plants. What have you got- three, four of them? We don't care much, but we will, if you don't do a little something for us."

"I don't now what you're talking about, "I said again, controlled this time, "And you," I added louder, waggling my big finger at Timmons, "Calm the fuck down."

"Fuck up Black," Timmons shot back sulkily, kicking the floor with his toe cap.

"Get out of my fuckin' face!" I said, losing it slightly, and stepping towards the side of the counter.

"Alright, enough!" said Merritt firmly; I think as much to Timmons, as to me.

"Okay, I don't know what yous are fucking talkin' about, but say what yous came to say," I offered, placing my hands flat on the counter. I could see drops of perspiration forming and I hoped they didn't notice.

"We just want some information Jimmy, that's all," said Merritt smoothly, starting his pitch.

"You're in a pretty unique position," chimed in Timmons, trying a less hostile tone and tac, "We know you're not paramilitary, and the most you do is sell a little grass, knock out a few dickheads once in a while. But your family."

He left that there.

"What about my fucking family?" I asked, my patience starting to fail again.

I was a bit rattled too. They were still cops after all- and they had some dirt on me, so I'd have to try and keep my cool.

Merritt took over again,

"Look, we're not going to ask you to betray anyone or anything like that," he said, gesturing heavily, "we're not interested in you family as such. We know who they are, but that's not what this is about."

I admit I was baffled about what they *did* want. It could have been the adrenaline shooting through me, disabling my thought processing, but I was bloody confused. And worried. What kind of a shake down was this?

"What do you fucking want then?" I asked quietly.

"Jimmy," started Merritt, leaning against the counter, talking as if we were two old acquaintances; shooting the shit in the bar, "Do you read the papers?"

Chapter 4

I shut the shop up when it got to lunch time. I took a half an hour over at *The Pitstop Café*, up off the Rathgael Road roundabout. I mechanically wolfed down my seven piece fry, thinking about the two peelers from earlier on. They had gone on to say how they were investigating some recent murders, all taking place around Belfast and North Down. I had read about two lads in recent weeks getting killed and I knew that both had been connected. I thought that had been a coincidence or just some infighting with the boyos. Details about the third body hadn't been released yet. What connected all three was the fact that each man had had a large part of skin peeled off from one of their fingers. It could have been down to torture, but the funny thing was that the fucker had removed it post mortem.

"You're not to go telling anyone this," Merritt had said, lowering his voice, "The most recent murder is of Bestie Nine-mill."

I had been genuinely shocked and it takes a lot to fucking shock me.
My instinct was to smile for some reason,

"No fucking way. I hear Bestie is over in England anyway. He's been doing some business deal or something," I shrugged then, "You know, ya hear things. Nobody's gonna take out Bestie "

Merritt regarded me coldly and shook his head,

"It's definitely him, it all checks out. DNA, you name it. It took a while to be sure- his head was near ripped off and the rest of him wasn't great looking either."

"Fucking hell," I had said, leaning back from the counter, "It can't be him," I looked at the floor, "He's meant to be over on business surely? Who'd be stupid enough? He could be negotiating for the DUP with the Tories for all I know- but no one would be stupid enough to off him. They'd have all the boys out after them."

"Well someone fucking did," broke in Timmons, looking all pleased with himself.

I regarded him coolly, like a toddler who's just thrown his food at you.

"Fuck off Tiny Tim," I said.

I played around with the last of my fried egg, prodding it with my fork, and reflected on how there was almost a scuffle between me and Timmons. Merritt had kept things calm. It wouldn't have done well to assault an officer of the law, on top of whatever else they knew about. I don't know why I got angry, I didn't particularly care for Nine-mill. I suppose I respected him in a way. He was part of the old school institution; he commanded your respect or he'd commandeer your knees. I thought back to the day me and my brother had sat next to him, as he threateningly polished that gun of his. I was just surprised that someone had the nerve to hit him. I set my fork down and thought back to watching them leave my shop, relief having brushed over me. A lonesome customer had sauntered in, then they quietly told me they'd be in touch and that all I had to do was keep my ears open, and gently push a few questions around here and there. I told them I could do that. What else could I do, except go to jail?

I sat back in the hard wooden chair and readied myself to go back to work. I became aware of two young girls, chatting at a table near by. To be fair, I could best describe them as a couple of wee millies.

“You going out the night Carly?” asked the first one, broad as you like.

“No money. Spent all my spares on this here,” said the other, grabbing her own peroxide curls with a scowl, “Fuckin’ disgrace, themins are usually good. My heart’s broke”

“Who done it for ya love- Stevie Wonder?”

I let out a smile, the old ones are the best.

Anyway, I wanted to know what these murders were all about and I was happy to do a bit of digging for them. I just wouldn’t necessarily tell them whatever I found out.

Chapter 5

"Rub my feet," said Pavla.

"No, you've got hairy toes," I replied.

She bounced up from our huddle on the sofa.

"I fucking do not!" she protested, slapping my arm.

"I'm only gegging love," I said, "Make me a cuppa?"

"You can get me a bloody tea," she said, pouting. When she said 'bloody', it sounded somewhere in between Yorkshire and South Africa. I found it endearing. I'm a big softie.

"If you switch off this fucking *Love Island* bullshit I will."

She considered this.

"We could watch a movie?"

"Deal," I said.

While the kettle was boiling, I made a phone call.

"How you doing Jimmy?" Leo said, answering after a few rings.

"Not bad buddy, look, are we okay talking on this line?"

"Yeah, should be fine," he said sounding hesitant, "Just don't go confessing to anything much; like killing J.F.K… or J.R."

"Yeah, okay, look," I said, pacing out of the kitchen and into the hall as the kettle began to hiss too noisily, "I've got some info for ya. You know that body that turned up a couple of days ago- had the fucked up finger?"

"Yeah, uhuh" he said gruffly.

"I've been told that it's Bestie Nine-mill."

He went silent for a moment and I paused, licking my lips.

"Bestie's meant to be in England. You sure?" he asked quietly.

"Yeah, my guy is reliable."

Me and Leo weren't really all that close and I wasn't about to tell him that I was talking to the cops.

"Fuck," he said simply.

"I know. I thought you'd want to know."

"Yeah, yeah, thanks Jim," he said absently, "Who told you?"

"I'm sorry, I can't tell ya Leo."

"Aww c'mon, for fucksake," he said, more pleading than angry.

"I can't, I'm sorry. Will this mean much hassle for you?"

"I suppose. Yeah, if it's definitely right. Shit."

There was an awkward pause.

"Well thanks Jim, here I'd better go make a few calls."

"Okay, no probs. You didn't hear it from me- okay?"

"Okay Jim, I'll ring you again, cheers."

"Alright Leo, see you later."

That was done, I'd keep the fuzz sweet, might as well try and forget about it. Things would be alright. I brought in a bottle of wine with the teas and a couple of DVD's. Pavla looked up at me, looking pleased, then suspicious.

"We're not having sex tonight," she said.

Chapter 6

I put an inaccurate 'Back in 5 minutes' sign on the shop door and drove up to *Shorter's Garage* in Ards, about eleven the next morning. My buddy Benny was a mechanic there.

"Bout ya Jim," he said, his gnarly, oil stained paw grabbing my hand.

"How you doing Benny, mate?" I replied.

The hairy man mountain made even me look undersized.

"You time for a chat?" I asked.

"Yeah, he said," scratching at his unkempt beard, leaving an oily residue behind, "I'm on my own today, Big Wayno's off on his holidays. He's gettin' an early bit of wreckin' in before the twelfth," Benny added, with a throaty chuckle.

He made us a cup of char and we sat on two old wooden sun chairs out on the front gravel. It was a dundering in old garage, up a steep path by the new industrial estate. The *'Shorter's Garage'* sign had long lost a *G* and an *A*, but Benny assured me they both like it better that way. The sun was out and I squinted as I flicked ash from my cigarette into his big plastic ash tray. It said 'Smithwicks' on it, which was only just legible, beneath the oily grime. I wondered how many years had gone by since one of them had swiped it from some rathole or another. We chatted for a bit and then I got down to business. Benny and his boss had fixed up cars nice and quiet for the boys for years- whatever needed doing before or after some dodgyness. Benny had gotten friendly with a lot of them too and I know he met up socially now and again. He just wasn't a paramilitary as such- I suppose a wee bit like myself.

"So here, I'm looking into something for a mate," I began, "It's to do with these murders, 'yon ones with the fucked up fingers."

Benny's big brown eyes seemed to glaze over for a moment and look past me.

"Yeah it's pretty mad that whole thing," he agreed and blew out his cheeks.

He didn't take the cue.

"I wanted to see if you knew anything?" I pushed, giving a shrug.

He lifted his tea and swigged it back and ran his hand through his thick hair, revealing a few greys.

"Sorry Jim- haven't heard nothin'. It sure is a weird one."

I looked at him squarely,

"Ya know they found another one a few days back? Haven't said who it is yet though."

"Have they? I hadn't heard."

I looked at him, hadn't heard? It was the fucking talk of the town.

"Yeah, it's all a wee bit feckin' grim," I said, "But if you hear anything?"

"Sure Jim, course," he replied, trying to sound enthusiastic, "no bother bud."

Maybe he just didn't like getting involved in that kind of shit or he didn't want me carrying anything back to me bro. It was just a bit weird.

"Cheers Benny, that'd be sweet."

"Better be getting back Jim," he said, getting heavily to his feet.

"Okay."

Chapter 7

That night was uneventful- for me anyway. I slept contentedly enough, but during my sleep, unbeknownst to me, a voicemail was left on my phone. I didn't get it till the next morning. It was from my old mate Stevie. He didn't sound himself;

> "Jim, it's me mate. I gotta speak to you about something…look, it's not good. I can't talk on this thing- look ring me- tonight if you can. See ya."

Later that day I found out he was dead.

Chapter 8

"What'dya mean he's dead? Are you fuckin' messing with me?"

Timmons didn't react as I got up in his face, he actually looked a little sorry for me this time.

Merrit cut in between us again and said,

"I know yous two were mates. I'm sorry. We need to get the bastard who's doing this."

My breathing felt heavy and I had to force myself to calm the fuck down. That's how I found out; from those two. They soon drifted out again, then there was a haze, and the rest of the morning was a blur. I locked the shop door and sat inside and cried.

"I'm sorry love, I'm sorry," is what I can remember Pav saying to me later that day, stroking my arm.

We just sat that afternoon in our front room, huddled up on the sofa. He was one of my best mates and he was dead. Not just dead, and not even just murdered. He was fucking beaten, his throat cut and the skin from one of his fingers removed. I just sat there and let her stroke me and I let the pain lap up from inside me and spill out, just a little. But what I promised myself right there, was that I would find the bastard responsible and I would make him sorry. I'd also make him say he was sorry, and then I'd kill him.

Chapter 9

Three weeks passed and 'The Twelfth' passed too. It went off peacefully enough- well, as peacefully as you can ever expect it to. I had spent much of my spare time taking to old friends and acquaintances, trying to find some link between the murders. Most seemed to have no idea or pretended not to. All the talk was about who had killed Bestie Nine-mill. Every day, the T.V news and local papers had something about his death. The rest of the dead were overshadowed; including my best mate.

"What's with the tabloids sayin' that the murders aren't really linked, and that the finger cutting could just be a new paramilitary trend- like sending a message or something?" I asked.

"I don't know Jim, I can't tell them what to write or broadcast. But, I'd prefer they didn't think they were linked anyhow," said Merritt soberly.

They had let me alone for a week or two, but had called in early again one morning. I guess they'd figured I'd had long enough to grieve. Or perhaps just the right amount.

"You're not startin' to think they're not?" I continued.

"No, of course they're linked," said Timmons, shaking his head dismissively.

I glared at him, "So why do yous care about the press?"

"I don't want the public to panic," Merritt said plainly, holding his hands up.

He began to pace and then lifted up a few records from the shelf and started to shuffle them into a neater position, "They most definitely are linked and not just that- they're all done by the same person."

He looked at me absently, then his brow creased.

“How can you be sure? Like DNA?” I asked.

“No, not that. They haven’t left any trace of anything. He’s thorough.”

“Just take our word for it, for fucksake,” barged in Timmons irately.”

“Fuckin’ bell end,” I muttered under my breath, not rising to it this time.

“There’s no doubt it’s one killer Jimmy,” continued Merritt, “All of our experts are certain. But beyond that- we just have no idea who he is.”

Merritt caught his subordinate’s eye and then looked away again. His voice was quieter;

“Jim, I shouldn’t be tellin’ you this much, but we need all the help we can get. We’re gonna need more from you.”

“I’ve been tryin’. I’ve been tryin’ everywhere. I wanna get the fucking fella,” I shouted, emotions rising up again. I forced them down.

He stopped and examined my face.

“Alright, I hear you. I just think that this guy will go on and on. Listen Jim,” he paused, “We have a lot of experts working on this. All sorts of guys. They tell me he’s a serial killer.”

He let it sit a moment. He paused and glanced at Timmons again, Timmons’s own face offered nothing.

“They tell me that this guy is *most definitely* a serial killer. That’s dangerous. They tell me he’s clever- that’s very dangerous. But I know he can be caught- just like anyone else. But, they tell me he doesn’t leave any clues. We’ve got basically nothin’. All we have is that all of the deaths involve guys involved with paramilitaries. What I don’t know is why.”

Chapter 10

"It's been too long again Jim," my brother said, shifting himself into the booth.

This time we had chosen *The Goat's Toe* in Bangor. It was the first I'd seen him since Stevie's funeral.

"It has," I agreed, and sipped my Harp, while scrutinising his face. I was pretty pissed off that he hadn't made much of an effort.

We were up on the roof garden and it was just starting to get busy. We sat at the long drinks table, up from the converted caravan-come smoking shelter. It was pretty cool. I kept looking at him, I didn't have anything to say.

"What?" he said, gesturing defensively, but letting out a laugh.

"It's nathin' much," I said.

Truth be told, I didn't quite know what exactlywas bothering me, or what I was really thinking about.

"Look, I know I should have made more time for ya," he said, squirming on the hard wood, "but since the whole Nine-mill thing came out- things have been hectic."

"I'm sure," I said, "I understand Lee," my voice softening, "would just like to see you more now and again."

"I know, and you will. I think things'll settle down soon," he said, and undid the buttons on his jacket. His beer paunch became more visible beneath his wrinkled shirt.

"Another new jacket?" I asked, raising an obvious eyebrow.

"It is- so what- 'bout time you smartened up- like I said the last time."

"Feck aff," I said and lit up a smoke.

Leo followed suit.

"But yeah, I have bought some new threads. Truth is that Nine-mill's death," he paused and lowered his voice, "his death had got me what you'd say are a few 'promotions.' I wasn't lookin' for them though, just how it goes. Means I'm busier."

"How you findin' it?"

"Alright. It's going okay- just a lot to sort out at the moment. The guys a few rungs up are clambering over each other- if ya know what I mean?"

"Yeah."

"I'm happy just to sit tight and keep my head down."

He sucked hard on his cigarette, and gazed beyond the beer garden and out towards the two sets of church spires. The quiet moment was interrupted when a drunk, two tables up; fell of his stool and crashed down onto the floor. There was a hush as he clambered to stand up and then as an afterthought; he gave a little bow.

"Yeoooo," followed a loud a roar from the surrounding rabble.

"Twat," I whispered to Leo.

The next hour or two passed quietly enough. The only further excitement was when some huffy bit threw her engagement ring at her boyfriend. It dropped down beneath the decking and all drama broke loose. A manager with a hammer and a screwdriver didn't manage to rectify it, and the unhappy couple were told they'd have to wait until Monday to try and get it back. Leo winked at me as they ambled down the aisle past us and left. We both were half liquored up by then and I spun the conversation round more directly to the murders. I suppose I wanted to pump him a bit for any info.

"So what's your take on it? Who the fuck do you think did it?" I asked, leaning in.

"Shit, I really dunno," he said, having difficulty getting his lighter to spark up another smoke, "It's really weird. All I can think of dat some dickheads from the other group are trying to push us. Take down the big dog ya'know? I just don't know why they haven't owned up yet. Could be they're planning another big move. Fuck 'em. Fuck da lot of 'em! We've got our own plans though Jim," he said, and looked hazily satisfied.

I don't know if it was his cig finally catching or something else.

We shared a taxi home around midnight and it dropped him off first.

"Out towards Scrabo," I said to the driver as he pulled away from Leo's house, after our drunken farewells.

I watched Leo as he struggled down the path to his house. He took out his mobile to make a phone call as he approached his front step. I shook my head and watched the trees and gates pass quickly, as the driver nipped up to a full thirty, back up the cul-de-sac. It always feels faster in the dark and the quiet of night. There's something about being all lit up within the dark too; more exposed.

"Stop here please mate," I blurted out abruptly, just before the turn at the end.

"You alright mate?" asked the driver.

"Yeah, just a bit sick, I uh, can take it from here- keep the change."

I bundled him a fiver and got out. As he sped off I started to amble slowly, but determinedly, back towards Leo's.

What was I doing? What did I want to ask him? Did I think Leo had something to do with things?

Did I think my brother was a serial killer?

No- he was many things, but not that. Yeah- he had actually probably killed people- but not like that. But something wasn't right. I knew that. I knew *him*- I'd known his lies and his tells since we were boys, running around the estate. He was hiding something. As I closed the gap, I felt my sweat becoming sticky in the pits of my T-shirt. I stopped by a tree, two doors before his house, in the most discreet position I could think of. I didn't exactly have all my wits about me. I lit up a cigarette and waited. What was I waiting for? I soon felt too cold, tired and stupid. I realised the drink had gotten the better of me and that I getting on like I was a bargain basement Humphrey Bogart chasing a Malteser Falcon. I turned to go and almost hit straight into the body stepping quickly towards me.

"What are ya hanging around out here for?" demanded a gravely, Antrim gulder.

"What the fuck is it to you?" I snarled back to the bulldog face that was barking at me.

He looked stocky and tight, but I was the size of an Irish Hound compared to him. His eyes were flaring, but then suddenly uncertain.

"Fucksake Jimmy, it's you."

I squinted hard at the now smiling face.

"Jesus, Freddie Workman," I said realising who it was.

"Sorry Jim- just saw someone hanging about and had to check. How the hell are ya?"

"You're grand, good to see you- it must be, what?"

"… six years. Well that's how long I was inside any road."

"Shit- so you doing security for my big bro?"

"Aye, yeah, that's it. I've been out a few months now- meant to look you up."

"No bother- look I better get headin' on- fuckin' steaming."

"What you doing out here anyway Jim," he asked, as I went to go past him, his eyes questioning again.

"Aww, we had been out for drinks and the taxi was making me feel sick, so I hopped out. Just catching my breath. Didn't wanna puke on the guy's seat."

"Shit, well sure I'll just say to Leo and then I'll run you home."

"No, no, I'm alright" I said and patted him firmly on the arm.

I turned and started up the road,

"Good to see you Freddie. The walk'll do me good, see you about," I said, turning on my heel to look at him.

"Alright Jim, sure thing," he said.

Chapter 11

"Hello?" I said into my phone, not recognising the number.

"Hello Jim."

I was sitting in 'Subway' the next morning, treating myself to a sausage bap and flat white.

"Is that you Benny?"

"Yeah," he continued, flatter than my flat white, "Listen Jim, I was thinkin' 'bout Stevie and everything and I… shit," he said pausing, "Fuck Jim, I shouldn't be talkin' to you."

I sat up straight and pushed my sarnie to one side.

"Benny," I said calmly, "Anything you tell me- I appreciate it and here- I won't say fuck all to anyone."

I waited as he breathed out a couple of times.

"Okay, right, I'm sayin' nuthin' more than this and I don't know nuthin' for definite. I've got no proof, just some things I've heard. I'm just giving you a name. After that, I'd best not talk to ya for a while okay?"

"Okay, thank you Benny, tell me," I said, trying to hold my nerve.

"Freddie Workman," he said and hung up.

I sat there looking at the stem rising off my coffee and a thin smile crept over my face. I don't know why.

The rest of the day flew in and for some reason I felt better than I had done in weeks. I shouldn't have really- if it was Freddie who was killing people- then my brother was probably involved too, or at least knew about it. Pavla made a stir fry for tea and I gobbled it up, along with a couple of tinnies. We got Skye bathed and down and the pair of us collapsed on the sofa, in front of an old repeat of 'Friends.' We half watched it, holding hands, Pav playing around on Facebook, as the cast played exaggerated versions of the characters they had played a few seasons before.

"I'm sorry if I'm been a moody bastard recently," I said.

She considered me and her eyes softened, as she rubbed up my arm.

"No Jimmy, you lost your friend."

I nodded.

"I love you," I said into her ear.

"I love you," she echoed back.

"Want me to make you some tea?" I asked.

"No, I need to send a few messages, I'll have one in a while, thank you baby."

"Okay, I'm gonna pop up for a quick smoke, be down in half an hour."

"Okay," she said, returning my smile.

I sat down with a piece of paper and a pen. I stuck a spliff in my mouth and fired on a side of Lee Morgan on the record player. I felt like fucking Carrie in Homeland. I scribbled some notes down as I tried to gather my thoughts. Could I be sure? What made most sense? I put those thoughts to the side for a moment and pictured my fists pummelling Workman's face into oblivion. I finished my smoke and then chewed on my pen. I had spent much of the afternoon in the shop, on the phone. I had rung a few particular mates, giving them various excuses and innocently dropped in a few questions about Workman. It seemed he had been out of prison for only a few months. That had correlated with the first murder. Seemingly he had been around about

Belfast during all the murders, so he had been in the right place to have done it. There was also a lot of talk about his violence and sometimes taking things too far. He couldn't be relied on for punishment beatings anymore- got carried away and that sort of thing. Then there's Benny giving me his name too- I just didn't know any of the whys. Why the killings? Well, according to Merritt whoever the murderer was- he was probably a psychopath. Why did I suspect my brother too? And what of? Was he using a psycho for his own ends? I finished another smoke and lit up a third. I checked the clock- best get back to Pavla soon. So- what- my bro was up to his neck in this? Yeah- that's exactly what I was thinking. Why not? Something was different about Leo. His reactions weren't quite right on a number of things. But what did that we really tell me? Hardly enough to give to the cops.

'Search for a new land' came to an end and I lifted the vinyl and carefully put it back in its sleeve. He was the one who seemed to be benefiting from it all. But where did that leave me? What would I do anyway- give my brother to the police? A paramilitary big shot at that. Put my family at risk too? Fuck no.

After we watched a movie, Pav went off to bed and I said I'd stay up a while. My mind was still racing. It was only after eleven and I thought I'd sink a few pints at my local before bed. It took five minutes for me to be in *Silver's*, with a pint of Guinness settling nicely in front of me. It was a dank hole, but a homely one. I greeted a few regulars I knew and then got stuck into my stout. Me and the two either side didn't speak until Big Paul with the ruddy face beside me shouted loudly to the barman,

"Cheers Phil, see you tomorrow," and then ambled out.

He always did that. He never said fuck all to anyone- but always gave a loud goodbye like the life and soul. I sat on for another one and there were only a few of us left in the bar. I knew them all more or less. There was a young guy working the bar, hadn't been there long- think it was Andy you called him.

"Gimme a mix," demanded a voice behind me. It was Raymond. He's alright- but a bit of twat when he's had a skinful.

"Sorry what's that?" said the kid politely.

"Gimme a mix," said Raymond, nastier and more slurred than before. He was big brute in his forties like me, though even more out of shape.

"I'm sorry what's in it?" tried the awkward teen again.

"Fucksake, he doesn't know how to pour fucking drinks," went off Ray, trying to get a laugh from someone, but not succeeding, "Get me someone who can make me a fuckin'drink," he added, getting his real nasty face on.

I stood up sharply,

"Excuse me buddy," I said to the kid, making sure he knew I was being friendly, "This prick wants a stupid fucking ladies drink of Bacardi and Vat 19, no ice and with a diet coke."

I paused to look at Ray and he started to fume. I smiled at him, but shot him a look to let him know I would be ready to fucking rumble. I continued to move behind the bar and started to fix his drink, this got a smile from the kid and a couple of laughs from the drunks in the room.

"There we are," I said, slapping it down on the bar and setting a crisp fiver beside it, "On me."

I went to return to my seat and then waggled my forefinger dramatically,

“Oh yeah, needs stirred,” I said and stuck my finger in and gave it a good stir. I licked it dry and then went back to my chair.

He looked raging, but just grabbed the drink and skulked off to a corner with it. Fuck ‘em.

Chapter 12

It bucketed constantly the next day. Feckin' pissing it down. When I just nipped out from the shop for fags, I got a soaking. Most of the customers that day were in sheltering from the rain and pretending they weren't; examining guitars and feigning an interest in some record sleeves. I sent an occasional glare and they sauntered out again, hoods up. I struggled with what to do all day. I had said nothing to Pav. What could I say without scaring her? 'By the way- I might be getting busted for dealing drugs you don't know about?' 'My brother might be mixed up with some serial killings?' Frig that. I got to the point in my head where I knew I couldn't wade in with my brother or Workman, without it ending shitty. I couldn't dig around much more either, without drawing attention. I also wasn't gonna tout on my brother. But I did want to be in the clear and I wanted something done about Stevie's death. So, it wasn't much of a jump to figure I'd offer the police what I knew, try and keep Leo out of it and take it from there. It seemed the best thing I could do.

"Hello Jimmy, I hope you have something for me."

"Yeah I do, as it goes."

"Good, 'cause I'm sorry but this offer won't last forever."

I felt impatient. I was the one ringing him.

"I fucking know who it is," I said and left it hanging.

"We should meet then," Merritt replied evenly.

"You wanna come by my shop after closing?"

"Aye, that'd to alright," he said, I thought trying to hide the extent of his interest, "So, how sure are you?"

"Pretty sure. Listen, I've got a lot of info for ya. But I want guarantees in return. I want nothin' coming back on me or my family, goes for my brother too."

"Hold your horses son," Merritt said firmly, his voice growing louder and more assured, "Let's just see what you have and we'll take it from there. We'll be the ones offering the deals- not you."

I bit on my lip,

"Well, just come by yourself anyway, don't be bringing that prick Timmons."

"Anything else?" he replied sarcastically, "Jesus Jimmy, you should be glad if I don't turn up with three squad cars and haul you in for questioning. Anyway, Timmons is a good man- asked 'specially to work on this case in the first place."

I didn't respond one way or the other and just blew out some air. Eventually he seemed to figure that was all my response was going to be.

"I was gonna ring you later anyway," he continued, "thought you might be interested in something. Let's keep things friendly- okay?"

"Yeah- 'course."

"Your old mate Davy Dick. When our team checked back on other loyalist murders, turns out he had had the skin taken off a finger too."

"Oh right?"

"Yeah. Maybe this was our guy's first one. Anyway, there it is. Right, your shop it is. See ya later, don't let me down," he said and rung off.

I sat and drummed my fingers on the counter, watching big rain drops bounce off my front window. I tried to keep in time with the falling droplets. I was spacing out. I set down the phone and ran my hand over my head. Something didn't feel right. Something was coming. I went and made a coffee and wolfed down a *Wispa*. That helped a bit. I went back to watching the rain. After a while it started to ease, but the hazy grey outside began to cover everywhere instead.

'Fuck,' I said out loud to myself, jolting. I remembered; Workman would have still been in jail when Davy was murdered.

Chapter 13

It had turned into a cool and dark summer's night by the time I locked the door. The rain lessoned, but seemed still to be falling in huge, slow drops. I sat and waited. When the outline appeared against the shop door and the bang on the glass followed, something looked wrong about it. I pulled the door open and was greeted by Timmons's hardened grimace.

"I wasn't expecting you," I said.

"I bet you weren't," he replied and pushed past, both his hands pressed deep down inside his raincoat.

I closed the door behind us and left the gentle splashing of the overflowing guttering to continue alone outside. I turned to see Timmons beginning to drip dry. His eyes were dancing wildly in his head. Oh yeah, in his right hand was a '38.

Chapter 14

"No fucking need that for that," I said, with a harder voice than was good for me.

"Stand over there," he commanded, gesturing to the space on the wall between some guitars on stands and a stacked up new Gretsch kit.

"I was expecting your partner," I said, my mind whirring inside my head.

I walked over slowly and turned, then leaned my back against the wall.

"Yeah, he's not gonna make it," he said, his eyes now boring into me, bulbous in their sockets.

I could feel my mind slowing in its revolutions, trying to make sense of this, clicking through spaces, trying to find something that fitted, searching to understand.

"There's no need for the gun, put it away and we can talk," I offered lightly.

"I don't think so," he said and his eyes darted about him, sizing the place up, "So, you know who's been killing the paramilitary scum do you? Well, well. And you told Meritt that I shouldn't come along?"

"Well, not exactly…" I said, my eyes narrowing.

"Quiet," he instructed, and tightened his grip on the gun for a moment, he licked his lips, "Your fucking brother spilled to you then I suppose, did he? Not such a big man after all," he shouted, though his voice quivered.

I said nothing. But I felt what I admit was akin to horror. I had inadvertently pissed of a psychopath and made him come to my shop to silence me.

"Wanker," I said quietly.

"What you fuckin' say?" he snapped and stepped closer. I could smell something foul on his breath.

"I said wanker. Not you- me. I'm a fucking wanker."

"Fuck off."

I wasn't really certain what I was doing- I was probably a bit wired with the whole situation.

"I'm a wanker," I continued, "I seem to have made you think I knew it was you. Funny thing is; I didn't. I though it was someone else."

"Bullshit," he rasped.

"It's actually true," I went on. Looking back- I suppose I was trying to rile him up, or just buy some time to think,

"That's what I was gonna tell Merritt. Where is Merritt by the way?"

His eyes almost rolled in his head and he shook his hair from near his eyes in a twitch, "You won't be talking to Merritt again," he said softly.

My face must have dropped.

"Your fault though Black!" he screamed suddenly, "He was a decent man."

I just nodded, understanding what he meant.

"It was Leo told you," he said in a whisper, pointing at me with his other hand, his head nodding to himself. A big finger hung inches from my face, as accusatory as Banquo's himself, "Well he'll be coming here soon too, and we'll see what's what, get this all cleared up."

He squinted up his eyes and rocked back on his heels. I chose my moment and suddenly scrambled down, grabbed the snare drum from the pile and heaved it into his face. It sent him flying back away from me. I would have preferred if it had been a bongo, but hey. It rattled and crashed as it rolled away, like a drunken drum roll. He regained his balance and the bugger managed to still keep the gun in his hand. I lunged at him, both my arms grabbing and batting down on his gun arm. I switched to punching his arm with my right fist and he let out a yelp, but came swinging back with his own right into my jaw. Fortunately he dropped the gun at the same time and I was able to take his punch easily enough. But then he rained down many more punches on me, like a Gorilla I had nicked a banana off of. I went down. I'm sure I could feel his sweat and spittle too, as I put my arms up in defence to the ferocity, trying to regain my balance on the floor. It was hurting, but I knew this angry tirade would ease as he tired. It seemed like an eternity as I felt new gashes opening up across my head and shoulders. But then he tired. I dragged myself up and grappled with him, trying to off balance him and gain the upper hand again. He stumbled backwards and the rage in his eyes also flickered fear. He tripped again and then I went to work. Right, right, right, left, right, left. Each one hit home hard and Timmons began to sway. He backed away, towards the vinyl shelves and couldn't get a proper block up. His nose was pissing blood all over the place. I kept on, my pulse raging through my body, exhilarated; right, right, left, right. He finally staggered badly and fell back against a shelf of records. Luckily there wasn't much good stuff on it. If he had fallen on my new Blue Note reissues- I'd have finished him. He lay on the ground, breathing hard; bleeding, and barely conscious. I allowed myself a second to breathe too; then went back to fetch the gun.

"Stop!"

I looked up to see Leo, with the gun in his hand. He had slipped in quietly through the back way.

"Stop what?" I shouted resentfully.

But he was looking past me.

I snapped round to see Timmons was on his feet and staggering towards me, a knife in his hand. My left ear seemed to implode, then fell deaf as the gun cracked off beside me. Timmons crumpled to the ground, a few feet away; with two slugs in him. Leo paced past me, his expression unreadable- to me anyhow. Timmons was still alive, as he looked up at my brother, bleeding heavily from the wounds in his chest. Leo swiftly pressed the gun to Timmons's forehead and pulled the trigger.

Chapter 15

Leo swivelled round to look at me and the gun hung loosely at his side. I didn't know in that moment if he was a friend or an enemy, a brother, or stranger.

"I think you got him." I said squarely.

Leo exhaled slowly. He slipped the gun into his back pocket and plucked out a cigarette.

"There's a smoking ban you know," I said as he lit up. He ignored me.

He looked down at the body and simply said, "Fuck."

We looked at each other, each trying to gauge the other. Each pretending we knew what to do or what was going to happen. Both failing to inspire any confidence- just like when we were stupid kids. I wiped at my head and covered it in a dusting of my own blood.

"Why did you have to get involved Jimmy?" he asked quietly, but with a hint of contempt in it.

"Why did you have to kill my best mate?" I countered, "You're a fucking animal," I added, the anger bubbling over.

"What do you know about?" he spat, "He's the animal," he said and gave the cadaver a kick.

"Shite!" he shouted, pacing on the spot, sucking hard on his cig.

"Why d'ya do it? Just for the money- the fucking cash? How did it start? '*Oh hello I see you're a psychopath, wanna work for me?*" I mocked.

"Something like that," he said with disinterest, just staring at the floor, thinking.

He began to pace about the room, as did I. His eyes followed my steps, studying me. It felt like a bull fight; the sparring at the beginning, the anticipation; but I didn't know who the matador was.

He breathed out hard again suddenly, "We had had a business arrangement going for a long time, lots of stuff. We were valuable to each other. I had a few guys lined up who could take the rap for things if needs be. Timmons was very useful to me. I'd spread a few rumours around every so often- bout a few lackeys just- who work for me. Timmons had a lot to lose and it wouldn't be good for me if he lost it- in any way. It wasn't until Davy Dick that he did a hit for me."

He stopped. He looked drained- old.

"You had Davy killed?"

"Yeah," he said simply, shrugging, "I saw something in him after that- a thirst. He wanted to do more- he liked it I suppose. He liked getting paid for it too, and it suited me."

"Suited you to kill everyone around you who caused you trouble? What about Stevie?"

He looked away.

"Stevie was a loose end. He knew too much- about the Davy stuff," he looked back at me, "Maybe he was a mistake, I don't know."

"Am I loose end too?" I said, pacing closer to him now.

"Shut up Jimmy, I need to think."

"Fuck yourself Leo," I said and we both stopped, facing one another, both faces like thunder.

Unexpectedly he reached into his back pocket and pulled out the gun. My eyes blazed and my body tensed. My brain was still flitting through what to do next, when he swivelled the gun in his hand and brought it crashing down on my head. Then everything slowly slipped away, trickling; like the blood running over my eyes, and there seemed to be no Jimmy left, just black.

Chapter 16

"I only like the green grapes. Fucking pips in 'em too."

"You ungrateful bastard," said Pav, leaning over my hospital bed and giving me a kiss, "You seem a bit better today."

She swiped the bag of red grapes away.

"Yeah, can't wait to get out of this bloody place," I said, struggling to loosen the starched sheets to sit up.

"Where's the wee woman," I asked, glancing to the door.

"I put her in an extra day of nursery."

I nodded, "I miss you love."

"You too," she said, and her eyes glistened, her face falling, "You need to look after yourself better."

"I know," I agreed, "Has there been anything on the news, my telly's on the blink again," I asked- nodding to my pay-as-you-watch set.

"No, nothing. It's still big news though. They think he's definitely skipped the country, but they don't know where."

I nodded again, I didn't know what to feel.

"It was the policeman's funeral today- Mr. Merritt," she added.

"Poor bugger," I said.

"It was big."

"I doubt there'll be many at Timmons's."

"No."

We both fell silent for a moment and Pav took my hand. I tried to take some kind of comfort that the worst must be over. But actually it wasn't.

If you enjoyed this e book, see other highly rated titles from

Simon Maltman on Amazon:

A Chaser on the Rocks- a bestselling psychological thriller novel

More Faces- a bestselling collection of 12 of Maltman's short stories

Facebook.com/simonmaltmancrimefiction

@simonmaltman